ANIMAL ARCHITECTS
BEES

by Karen Latchana Kenney

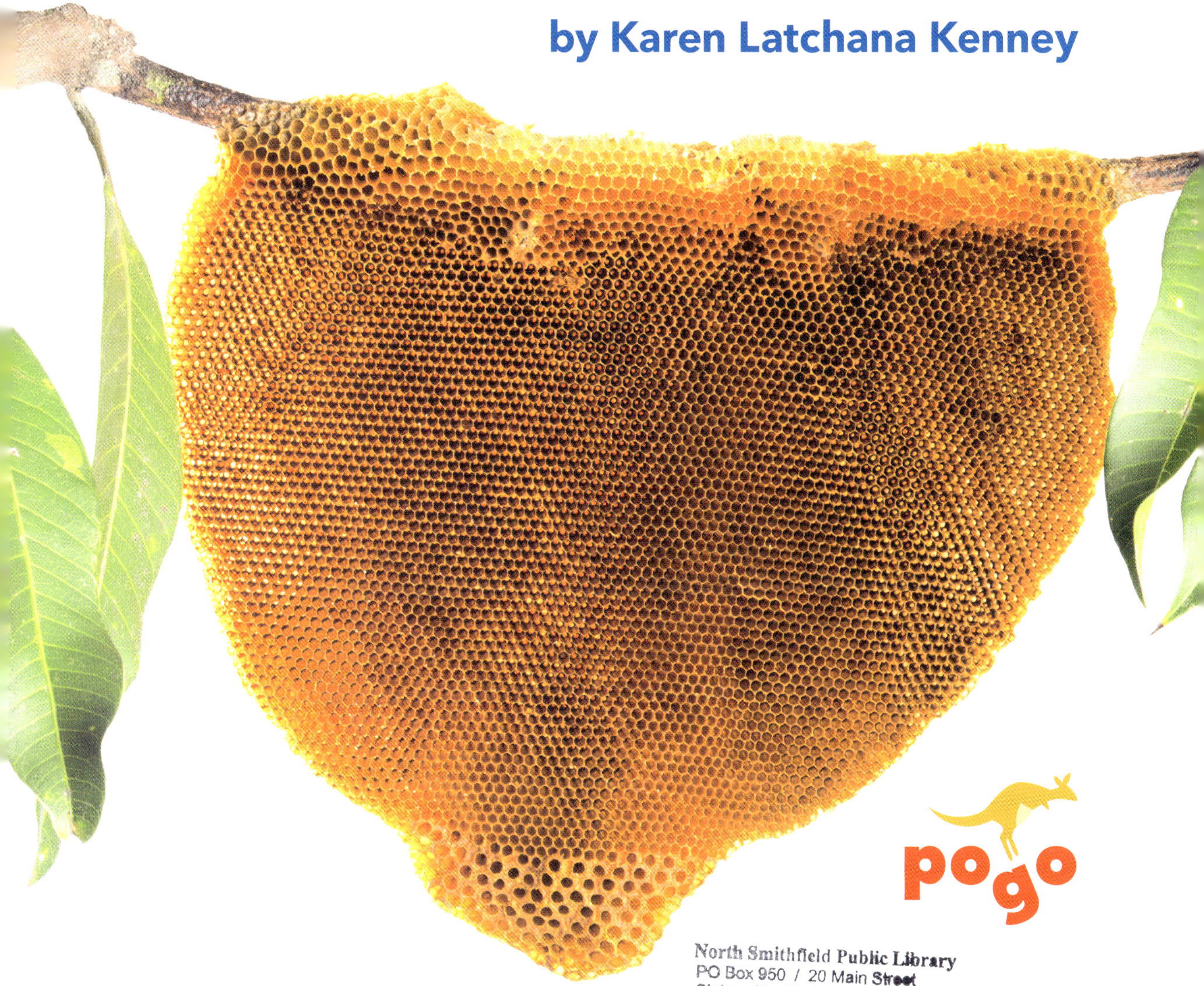

Ideas for Parents and Teachers

Pogo Books let children practice reading informational text while introducing them to nonfiction features such as headings, labels, sidebars, maps, and diagrams, as well as a table of contents, glossary, and index.

Carefully leveled text with a strong photo match offers early fluent readers the support they need to succeed.

Before Reading

- "Walk" through the book and point out the various nonfiction features. Ask the student what purpose each feature serves.
- Look at the glossary together. Read and discuss the words.

Read the Book

- Have the child read the book independently.
- Invite him or her to list questions that arise from reading.

After Reading

- Discuss the child's questions. Talk about how he or she might find answers to those questions.
- Prompt the child to think more. Ask: Have you ever seen a hive or another structure made by bees? Did you see the bees building it?

Pogo Books are published by Jump!
5357 Penn Avenue South
Minneapolis, MN 55419
www.jumplibrary.com

Copyright © 2018 Jump!
International copyright reserved in all countries.
No part of this book may be reproduced in any form without written permission from the publisher.

Library of Congress Cataloging-in-Publication Data

Names: Kenney, Karen Latchana, author.
Title: Bees / by Karen Latchana Kenney.
Description: Minneapolis, MN: Jump!, Inc., [2018]
Series: Animal architects | Audience: Ages 7-10.
Includes bibliographical references and index.
Identifiers: LCCN 2016050405 (print)
LCCN 2016051577 (ebook)
ISBN 9781620316931 (hardcover: alk. paper)
ISBN 9781624965708 (ebook)
Subjects: LCSH: Bees–Juvenile literature.
Bees–Habitations–Juvenile literature.
Classification: LCC QL565.2 .K458 2018 (print)
LCC QL565.2 (ebook) | DDC 595.79/9–dc23
LC record available at https://lccn.loc.gov/2016050405

Editor: Kirsten Chang
Book Designer: Michelle Sonnek
Photo Researcher: Michelle Sonnek

Photo Credits: Valentina Proskurina/Shutterstock, cover; Phundit Watanakasivish/Shutterstock, 1; Eric Isselee/Shutterstock, 3; Treat Davidson/Alamy Stock Photo, 4; Pakhnyushchy/Shutterstock, 5; thailoei92/Shutterstock, 6-7; Maciej Olszewski/Shutterstock, 8-9; suriyasilsaksom/Thinkstock, 10; Arco/age fotostock, 11; ANT Photo Library/Science Source, 12-13; Fabio Colombini Medeiros/age fotostock, 14-15; Zoonar/Alamy Stock Photo, 16-17; Agustin Esmoris/Shutterstock, 18-19; John M Coffman/Getty, 20; Perfect Lazybones/Shutterstock, 20; Barcroft Media/Getty, 21; Protasov AN/Shutterstock, 23.

Printed in the United States of America at Corporate Graphics in North Mankato, Minnesota.

3 5944 00139 3899

TABLE OF CONTENTS

CHAPTER 1
Wax Makers 4

CHAPTER 2
Nest Builders 10

CHAPTER 3
Bees in the World 20

ACTIVITIES & TOOLS
Try This! 22
Glossary 23
Index 24
To Learn More 24

CHAPTER 1
WAX MAKERS

Inside a **hive**, a honeybee builds a **cell**. First a liquid wax forms on its **abdomen**. It cools into scales. They look like fish scales.

scale

cell

The bee removes a scale and passes it to its mouth. It chews and mixes the wax with **saliva**. Then it adds the soft wax to the cell. It uses its **antennae** to shape it. Soon it will be a perfect **hexagon**.

CHAPTER 5

The strong cells fit together perfectly. Some hold honey and **pollen**. Other cells hold growing young bees.

A few thousand honeybees live in a **colony**. Their hive is made of layers of wax cells, called combs. The space between the combs is big enough for two bees. This gives them room to work.

> **DID YOU KNOW?**
>
> To make honey, bees collect flower **nectar**. They mix it with an **enzyme**. It changes the nectar into honey. Honey is an important food source for bees.

CHAPTER 1

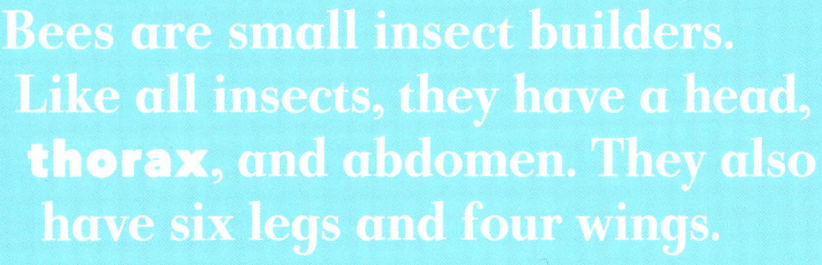

Bees are small insect builders. Like all insects, they have a head, **thorax**, and abdomen. They also have six legs and four wings.

Two antennae help bees sense things. They use their strong jaws to chew. Both help bees build.

DID YOU KNOW?

Near a hive, you can hear a steady buzz. This hum is made from bees' fast-beating wings.

CHAPTER 1   9

CHAPTER 2
NEST BUILDERS

Bees build **nests** for their homes and young. Some nests are hives. They may build hives on houses and in trees.

Some bees dig tunnels in the ground. Others make their nests in hollow plant stems.

Bees either work together or alone. Social bees live in large groups. A queen lays eggs. Worker bees build and take care of the hive.

Solitary bees live alone. Each bee builds its own nest. It lays eggs and leaves them alone to hatch.

DID YOU KNOW?

More than 20,000 kinds of bees live on Earth. Most are solitary bees.

CHAPTER 2

Stingless bees are social. They work together to make their nest inside a hollow tree. They mix wax with tree sap, **resin**, mud, or pulp. They use this material to make thick walls above and below the hive. The walls protect the hive.

Flat cell layers hold young bees. Larger wax cups hold honey and pollen. Some nests have a long tube leading outside. This is the bees' doorway.

TAKE A LOOK!

What does the inside of a stingless bee's nest look like?

- ■ = storage pots
- ■ = entrance
- ■ = cells

CHAPTER 2

queen

CHAPTER 2 15

Mining bees are solitary. A mining bee makes its nest underground. It digs tunnels and cells in the earth.

Its body produces a liquid, and it lines the walls with it. The liquid hardens. Now water won't leak into the nest.

The bee mixes the liquid, nectar, and pollen in each cell. This will be food for the larvae. It lays an egg in each cell. It seals the cells and flies away.

CHAPTER 2

TAKE A LOOK!

What does the inside of a mining bee's nest look like?

- = mound
- = soil
- = tunnels
- = cells
- = eggs

CHAPTER 2 17

Some bees make nests inside wood. A carpenter bee chooses dead wood. It uses its strong jaws to chew tunnels for its nest.

The bee makes a series of cells in a tunnel. It mixes sawdust with saliva to make the cell walls. Each cell holds food and a single egg.

TAKE A LOOK!

What does the inside of a carpenter bee's nest look like?

■ = tunnels
■ = walls
■ = cells

CHAPTER 2   19

CHAPTER 3
BEES IN THE WORLD

Sometimes carpenter bees pick houses for their nests. A hive on your house might cause problems. Bees can damage the wood. Bees also sting people if they come too close.

But some animals seek out beehives. Bears and honey badgers like to eat honey.

Busy bees build in many ways. Up in trees or underground, bees make amazing nests.

CHAPTER 3 21

ACTIVITIES & TOOLS

TRY THIS!

MAKE HONEYBEE CELLS

Try making honeybee cells with different shapes. Which works best?

What You Need:
- construction paper
- scissors
- ruler
- clear tape

❶ Cut 12 1×6-inch (2.5×10-centimeter) strips of construction paper.

❷ Fold six pieces into hexagon shapes. Tape the strips in place.

❸ Roll six pieces into circle shapes. Tape the strips in place.

❹ Fit the six hexagons together. Tape them in place. What do you notice about how they fit together?

❺ Fit the six circles together. Tape them in place. How do the circles fit together? Which do you think is a better design? Why?

GLOSSARY

abdomen: The back section of an insect's body.

antennae: Two long, thin parts on an insect's head that it uses to feel things.

cell: A small room in a nest or hive.

colony: A large group of insects that live together.

enzyme: A protein in an animal's body that causes chemical reactions.

hexagon: A shape with six sides.

hive: A structure filled with wax cells that is made by bees.

nectar: A sweet liquid that bees collect from flowers.

nests: Places built by animals and insects to have their young and live in.

pollen: Tiny yellow grains made by flowers.

resin: A sticky substance that oozes from certain trees.

saliva: A clear liquid in the mouth.

thorax: The section of an insect's body that is between its head and abdomen.

INDEX

abdomen 4, 9
antennae 5, 9
cell 4, 5, 6, 14, 16, 19
colony 6
combs 6
eggs 13, 16, 19
enzyme 6
hexagon 5
hive 4, 6, 9, 10, 13, 14, 20, 21
honey 6, 14, 21
honey badgers 21
jaws 9, 19
nectar 6, 16
nests 10, 11, 13, 14, 16, 17, 19, 20, 21
pollen 6, 14, 16
queen 13
saliva 5, 19
social 13, 14
solitary 13, 16
thorax 9
trees 10, 14, 21
tunnels 11, 16, 19
wax 4, 5, 6, 14
wood 19, 20

TO LEARN MORE

Learning more is as easy as 1, 2, 3.
1) Go to www.factsurfer.com
2) Enter "beearchitects" into the search box.
3) Click the "Surf" button to see a list of websites.

With factsurfer, finding more information is just a click away.

ACTIVITIES & TOOLS

2/2018 P 18
Creepy Crawly
595.799
Ken

North Smithfield Public Library

P Creepy Crawly 595.799 Ken
Kenney, Karen Latchana, author
Bees

35944001393899